Jennifer E. Smith is the author of *This Is What Happy Looks Like*, *The Statistical Probability of Love at First Sight*, *The Storm Makers*, *The Comeback Season* and *You Are Here*. Her work has been translated into twenty-nine languages. She earned a master's degree in creative writing from the University of St. Andrews in Scotland and currently works as an editor in New York City. Her website is jenniferesmith.com.

Praise for Jennifer E. Smith

'Packed with fun and romance . . . totally charming'
Closer

'Perfect' *Heat*

'Imagine a book version of *You've Got Mail*
but loads funnier' *Company*

'I read it in one sitting and when I finally put it down
I was beaming and a bit tearful . . . A sweet, charming,
romantic book' Keris Stainton

'An extraordinary look at chance, connections,
and the power of family and love' Elizabeth Scott

'That whole fresh, dizzy gorgeousness of first love is
there . . . Highly recommended!' Carmen Reid

'This high-flying romance will send your heart soaring'
Now

'This irresistible novel seems set to become one of
the most talked about books of the year' *Glamour*

'If you don't read this book in one sitting there may well
be something wrong with you . . . An absolute treat'
Cat Clarke

By Jennifer E. Smith and published by Headline

The Statistical Probability Of Love At First Sight
This Is What Happy Looks Like
The Geography of You And Me

THE GEOGRAPHY OF
YOU
AND
ME

JENNIFER E. SMITH

headline

First published in Great Britain in 2014
by HEADLINE PUBLISHING GROUP

First published in paperback in Great Britain in 2014
by HEADLINE PUBLISHING GROUP

1

Cataloguing in Publication Data is available from the British Library

ISBN 978 1 4722 0630 5

Offset in Plantin by Avon DataSet Ltd,
Bidford-on-Avon, Warwickshire

Printed and bound in Great Britain by
Clays Ltd, St Ives plc

Papers used by Headline are from well-managed forests
and other responsible sources.

HEADLINE PUBLISHING GROUP
An Hachette UK company
338 Euston Road
London NW1 3BH

www.headline.co.uk
www.hachette.co.uk

To Allison, Erika, Brian, Melissa, Meg, and Joe—
for being such great company
during the real blackout

PART I

Here

1

On the first day of September, the world went dark.

But from where she stood in the blackness, her back pressed against the brassy wall of an elevator, Lucy Patterson had no way of knowing the scope of it yet.

She couldn't have imagined, then, that it stretched beyond the building where she'd lived all her life, spilling out onto the streets, where the traffic lights had gone blank and the hum of the air conditioners had fallen quiet, leaving an eerie, pulsing silence. Already, there were people streaming out onto the long avenues that stretched the length of Manhattan, pushing their way toward home like salmon moving up a river. All over the island, car horns filled the air and windows were thrown open, and in thousands upon thousands of freezers, the ice cream began to melt.

The whole city had been snuffed out like a candle, but from the unlit cube of the elevator, Lucy couldn't possibly have known this.

Her first thought wasn't to worry about the violent jolt that had brought them up short between the tenth and eleventh floors, making the whole compartment rattle like a ride at an amusement park. And it wasn't a concern for their escape, because if there was anything that could be depended on in this world—far more, even, than her parents—it was the building's small army of doormen, who had never failed to greet her after school, or remind her to bring an umbrella when it was rainy, who were always happy to run upstairs and kill a spider or help unclog the shower drain.

Instead, what she felt was a kind of sinking regret over her rush to make this particular elevator, having dashed through the marble-floored lobby and caught the doors just before they could seal shut. If only she'd waited for the next one, she would've still been standing downstairs right now, speculating with George—who worked the afternoon shift—about the source of the power outage, rather than being stuck in this small square of space with someone she didn't even know.

The boy hadn't looked up when she'd slipped through the doors just a few minutes earlier, but instead kept his eyes trained on the burgundy carpet as they shut again with a bright *ding*. She'd stepped to the back of the elevator without acknowledging him, either, and in the silence that followed she could hear the low thump of music from his headphones as the back of his white-blond head bobbed, just slightly, his rhythm not quite there. She'd noticed him around before, but this was the first time it struck her how much he looked like a scarecrow, tall and lanky and loose-limbed, a study of lines and angles all jumbled together in the shape of a teenage boy.

He'd moved in just last month, and she'd watched that day from the coffee shop next door as he and his father carried a small collection of furniture back and forth across the gum-stained sidewalk. She'd known they were hiring a new superintendent, but she hadn't known he'd be bringing his son, too, much less a son who looked to be about her age. When she'd tried getting more information out of the doormen, all they could tell her was that they were somehow related to the building's owner.

She'd seen him a few more times after that—at the mailboxes or crossing the lobby or waiting for the bus—but even if she'd been the kind of girl inclined to walk up and introduce herself, there still was something vaguely unapproachable about him. Maybe it was the earbuds he always seemed to be wearing, or the fact that she'd never seen him talking to anyone before; maybe it was the way he slipped in and out of the building so quickly, like he was desperate not to be caught, or the faraway look in his eyes when she spotted him across the subway platform. Whatever the reason, it seemed to Lucy that the idea of ever meeting him—the idea of even saying something as harmless as *hello*—was unlikely for reasons she couldn't quite articulate.

When the elevator had wrenched to a stop, their eyes

met, and in spite of the situation, she'd found herself wondering—ridiculously—whether he recognized her, too. But then the lights above them had snapped off, and they were both left blinking into the darkness, the floor still quivering beneath them. There were a few metallic sounds from above—two loud clanks followed by a sharp bang— and then something seemed to settle, and except for the faint beat of his music, it was silent.

As her eyes adjusted, Lucy could see him frown and then pull out his earbuds. He glanced in her direction before turning to face the panel of buttons, jabbing at a few with his thumb. When they refused to light up, he finally hit the red emergency one, and they both cocked their heads, waiting for the speaker to crackle to life.

Nothing happened, so he punched it again, then once more. Finally, he lifted his shoulders in a shrug. "It must be the whole building," he said without turning around.

Lucy lowered her eyes, trying to avoid the little red arrow above the door, which was poised somewhere between the numbers 10 and 11. She was doing her best not to picture the empty elevator shaft below, or the thick cables stretched above them.

"I'm sure they're already working on it," she said, though she wasn't at all sure. She'd been in the elevator when it got stuck before, but never when the lights had gone out, too, and now her legs felt unsteady beneath her, her stomach wound tight. Already, the air seemed too warm and the space too small.

4

She cleared her throat. "George is just downstairs, so…"

The boy turned to face her, and though it was still too dark for details, she could see him more clearly with each minute that passed. She was reminded of a science experiment her class did in fifth grade, where the teacher dropped a mint into each of the students' cupped palms, then switched off the lights and told them to bite down hard, and a series of tiny sparks lit up the room. This was how he seemed to her now: his teeth flashing when he spoke, the whites of his eyes bright against the blackness.

"Yeah, but if it's the whole building, this could take a while," he said, slumping against the wall. "And my dad's not around this afternoon."

"My parents are away, too," Lucy told him, and she could just barely make out the expression on his face, an odd look in her direction.

"I meant 'cause he's the super," he said. "But he's just in Brooklyn, so I'm sure he'll be back soon."

"Do you think…?" she began, then paused, not sure how to phrase the question. "Do you think we're okay till then?"

"I think we'll be fine," he said, his voice reassuring; then, with a hint of amusement, he added: "Unless, of course, you're afraid of the dark."

"I'm okay," she said, sliding down the wall until she was sitting on the floor, her elbows resting on her knees. She attempted a smile, which emerged a little wobbly. "I've heard monsters prefer closets to elevators."

5

"Then I think we're in the clear," he said, sitting down, too, his back against the opposite corner. He pulled his phone from his pocket, and in the dim light, his hair glowed green as he bent his head over it. "No signal."

"It's usually pretty iffy in here anyway," Lucy said, reaching for her own phone before realizing she'd left it upstairs. She'd only run down to grab the mail, a quick round-trip to the lobby and back, and now it felt like a particularly bad moment to find herself completely empty-handed.

"So," the boy said, tipping his head back against the wall. "Come here often?"

She laughed. "I've logged some time in this particular elevator, yes."

"I think you're about to log a lot more," he said with a rueful smile. "I'm Owen, by the way. I feel like we should probably introduce ourselves so I don't end up calling you Elevator Girl whenever I tell this story."

"I could live with Elevator Girl," she said. "But Lucy works, too. I'm in 24D."

He hesitated a moment, then gave a little shrug. "I'm in the basement."

"Right," she said, remembering too late, and she was glad for the darkness, which hid the flush in her cheeks. The building was like a small country in and of itself, and this was the currency; when you met someone new, you didn't just give your name but your apartment number as well, only she'd forgotten that the super always lived in the

6

small two-bedroom flat in the basement, a floor Lucy had never visited.

"In case you're wondering why I'm on my way up," he said after a moment, "I've figured out that the view's a whole lot better on the roof."

"I thought nobody was allowed up there."

He slipped his phone back into his pocket and pulled out a single key, which he held flat in his palm. "That's true," he said with a broad grin. "Technically speaking."

"So you have friends in high places, huh?"

"Low places," he said, returning the key to his pocket. "The basement, remember?"

This time she laughed. "What's up there, anyway?"

"The sky."

"You've got keys to the sky?" she said, and he knitted his fingers together, lifting his arms above his head in a stretch.

"It's how I impress all the girls I meet in the elevator."

"Well, it's working," she said, amused. Watching him over the past weeks, studying him from afar, she'd imagined he must be shy and unapproachable. But sitting here now, the two of them grinning at each other through the dark, she realized she might have been wrong. He was funny and a little bit odd, which at the moment didn't seem like the worst kind of person to be stuck with.

"Although," she added, "I'd be a lot more impressed if you could get us out of here."

"I would, too," he said, shifting his gaze to scan the

ceiling. "You'd think the least they could do would be to pipe in some music."

"If they're planning to pipe in anything, hopefully it's some cool air."

"Yeah, this whole city's like a furnace," he said. "It doesn't feel like September."

"I know. Hard to believe school starts tomorrow."

"Yeah, for me, too," he said. "Assuming we ever get out of here."

"Where do you go?"

"Probably not the same place as you."

"Well, I hope not," she said with a grin. "Mine's all-girls."

"Then definitely not the same one," he said. "But I'd already figured that out anyway."

"What do you mean?"

"Well," he said, waving a hand around. "You live here."

Lucy raised her eyebrows. "In the elevator?"

"In this building," he said, making a face.

"So do you."

"I think it would be more accurate to say I live *under* this building," he joked. "But I'm betting you go to some fancy private school where everyone wears uniforms and worries about the difference between an A and an A-minus."

She swallowed hard, unsure what to say to this, since it was true.

Taking her silence as an admission, he tilted his head as if to say *I told you so*, then gave a little shrug. "I'm going to the one up on One Hundred and Twelfth that looks like a bunker, where everyone goes through metal detectors and worries about the difference between a C and a C-minus."

"I'm sure it won't be that bad," she said, and his jaw went tight. Even through the darkness, something about his expression made him seem much older than he'd looked just moments before, bitter and cynical.

"The school or the city?"

"Doesn't sound like you're too thrilled about either."

He glanced down at his hands, which were resting in a knot on top of his knees. "It's just...this wasn't really the plan," he said. "But my dad got offered this job, and now here we are."

"It's not so bad," she told him. "Really. You'll find things to like about it."

He shook his head. "It's too crowded. You can't ever breathe here."

"I think you're confusing the city with this elevator."

The corner of his mouth twitched, but then he frowned again. "There are no open spaces."

"There's a whole park just a block away."

"You can't see the stars."

"There's always the planetarium," Lucy said, and in spite of himself, he laughed.

"Are you always so relentlessly optimistic, or just when it comes to New York?"

"I've lived here my whole life," she said with a shrug. "It's my home."

"Not mine."

9

"Doesn't mean you have to play the sullen-new-guy card."

"It's not a card," he said. "I *am* the sullen new guy."

"Just give it a chance, Bartleby."

"*Owen*," he said, looking indignant, and she laughed.

"I know," she told him. "But you're sounding just like Bartleby from the story." She waited to see if he knew it, then pushed on. "Herman Melville? Author of *Moby-Dick*?"

"I know *that*," he said. "Who's Bartleby?"

"A scrivener," she explained. "Sort of a clerk. But throughout the whole story, anytime someone asks him to do something, all he says is 'I would prefer not to.'"

He considered this a moment. "Yup," he said finally. "That pretty much sums up my feelings about New York."

Lucy nodded. "You would prefer not to," she said. "But that's just because it's new. Once you get to know it more, I have a feeling you'll like it here."

"Is this the part where you insist on taking me on a tour of the city, and we laugh and point at all the famous sights, and then I buy an *I♥NY* T-shirt and live happily ever after?"

"The T-shirt is optional," she told him.

For a long moment, they eyed each other across the cramped space, and then, finally, he shook his head. "Sorry," he said. "I know I'm being a jerk."

Lucy shrugged. "It's okay. We can just chalk it up to claustrophobia. Or lack of oxygen."

10

He smiled, but there was something strained about it. "It's just been a really tough summer. And I guess I'm not used to the idea of being here yet."

His eyes caught hers through the darkness, and the elevator felt suddenly smaller than it had just minutes before. Lucy thought of all the other times she'd been crammed in here over the years: with women in fur coats and men in expensive suits; with little white dogs on pink leashes and doormen wheeling heavy boxes on luggage carts. She'd once spilled an entire container of orange juice on the carpet right where Owen was sitting, which had made the whole place stink for days, and another time, when she was little, she'd drawn her name in green marker on the wall, much to her mother's dismay.

She'd read the last pages of her favorite books here, cried the whole way up and laughed the whole way down, made small talk to a thousand different neighbors on a thousand different days. She'd fought with her two older brothers, kicking and clawing, until the door *ding*ed open and they all walked out into the lobby like perfect angels. She'd ridden down to greet her dad when he arrived home from every single business trip, and had even once fallen asleep in the corner as she waited for her parents to come home from a charity auction.

And how many times had they all been stuffed in here together? Dad, with his newspaper folded under his arm, always standing near the door, ready to bolt; Mom, wearing a thin smile, seesawing between amusement and impatience

11

with the rest of them; the twins, grinning as they elbowed each other; and Lucy, the youngest, tucked in a corner, always trailing behind the rest of the family like an ellipsis at the end of a sentence.

And now here she was, in a box that seemed too tiny to hold so many memories, with the walls pressing in all around her and nobody to come to her rescue. Her parents were in Paris, across the ocean, as usual, on the kind of trip that only ever included the two of them. And her brothers—the only friends she'd ever really had—were now thousands of miles away at college.

When they'd left a few weeks ago—Charlie heading off to Berkeley, and Ben to Stanford—Lucy couldn't help feeling suddenly orphaned. It wasn't unusual for her parents to be away; they'd always made a habit of flying off to snow-covered European cities or exotic tropical islands on their own. But being left behind was never that bad when there were three of them, and it was always her brothers—a twin pair of clowns, protectors, and friends—who had kept everything from unraveling.

Until now. She was used to being parentless, but being brotherless—and, thus, effectively friendless—was entirely new, and losing both of them at once seemed unfair. The whole family was now hopelessly scattered, and from where she sat—all alone in New York—Lucy felt it deeply just then, as if for the very first time: the bigness of the world, the sheer scope of it.

Across the elevator, Owen rested his head against the